WITNESS

'Todd Lucas!'

A year twelve was walking towards him.

'I got a message for you from my cousin,' she said. 'His name's Stephen Ripley. He says you know his brother.'

Stephen Ripley? Todd didn't know anyone of that name. Then he remembered. Ripley. Jason Ripley. The man who attacked Mr Wilson.

'What's the message?' Todd said.

'Stephen said you'll be seeing him. Sooner than you think.'

SHARP SHADES

WITNESS

Look out for other exciting stories
in the *Sharp Shades* series:

SHARP SHADES
WITNESS

Anne Cassidy

Published by Evans Brothers Limited
2A Portman Mansions
Chiltern St
London W1U 6NR

British Library Cataloguing in Publication Data
Cassidy, Anne, 1952-
  Witness. - Abridged ed. - (Sharp shades)
  1. Crime - Fiction 2. Witnesses - Fiction
  3. Young adult fiction
  I. Title
  823.9'14[J]

ISBN 9780237534462

Series Editor: David Belbin
Editor: Julia Moffatt
Designer: Rob Walster
Picture research: Bryony Jones

This abridged edition was first published in its
original form as a *Shades* title of the same name.

Picture acknowledgements:
istockphoto.com: pp 8, 17, 23, 27, 35, 41, 45, and
49. Bryony Jones: pp 14, 42 and 53.

Contents

Chapter One
Late Again

Todd Lucas was late for school
when he saw the attack. It was a
wet Monday morning. He was
sending a text message to Dex, his
best mate.

A loud crash made him jump. He spun round and saw a window shatter. A man burst out of Wilson's Food and Wines. He was tall and well built and wore a short leather zip-up jacket. He stopped and looked around. He saw Todd. Todd was sure he knew the man. The man walked quickly on. Todd tried to remember the man's name. Then Mr Wilson staggered out of the shop.

'Stop! You, stop!' he shouted. 'I've rung the police. They're coming.'

The man turned round. He

marched back to Mr Wilson. He grabbed the old man by his tie.

'I told you to shut up!' he hissed.

The man pulled one arm back. He punched Mr Wilson. Mr Wilson fell to the ground. The man ran away. Todd hurried to Mr Wilson. Now he remembered the attacker. He used to be assistant caretaker in his primary school. Jason Ripley.

Todd knelt down. The old man's eyes opened and closed. Blood ran from his nose. He had no idea where he was.

'It's all right, Mr Wilson,' Todd said. 'It's me, Todd Lucas. I used to do a paper round for you.'

Todd took his mobile out and pressed 999.

'Ambulance,' he said. 'Quick as you can.'

Chapter Two
Being a Grass

'Just sign there,' PC Roberts said.

Todd signed the piece of paper. Then he looked at his watch. Eleven ten. He was really late for school.

'You did well,' PC Roberts said.

'We know this Jason Ripley and his family. It won't be long before we pick him up.'

PC Roberts put the statement into a pink folder. Todd checked his mobile. Three missed calls.

'I don't want anyone to know about this,' he said.

'Completely confidential,' PC Roberts said. 'You should be proud of yourself. You did the right thing.'

Todd knew it wasn't as simple as this. He wasn't a grass. He wasn't exactly a saint himself. Life was easier if you didn't get involved.

Mr Wilson was different. Todd

had worked for him. He liked him.
On payday he gave Todd free
magazines. His wife, Mrs Wilson,
was always singing along with the
radio. His son, Terry, had been to
every single West Ham football
game for twenty years. Mr Wilson
didn't deserve to be beaten up
in the street.

Todd got on the bus and sat by a
window. He remembered when Jason
Ripley worked in his school. He was
always in a bad mood.

The bus stopped and he got off.
He hurried towards the back gate.

'Todd!' a voice called. He turned

round. Louise, Lindy and Dex were behind him. Louise and Lindy held camcorders. Dex had a clipboard and a pen.

'Where you been?' Louise shouted.

'Sssh...' Todd said. 'I'll tell you later.'

He joined them. Now he stood between two six-foot tall, black girls and a small, thin, white boy with

giant glasses. The whole school would see them.

Next day Todd and Dex were early for once.

'Louise likes you,' Dex said.

'I know,' Todd said.

'No, I mean she lusts after you.'

Todd liked Louise. She was funny and chatty and knew tons about football. Every now and again she stood a little too close to him. It made him feel awkward.

'Todd Lucas!'

A year twelve was walking towards him.

'I got a message for you from my cousin,' she said. 'His name's Stephen Ripley. He says you know his brother.'

Stephen Ripley? Todd didn't know anyone of that name. Then he remembered. Ripley. Jason Ripley. The man who attacked Mr Wilson. 'What's the message?' Todd said.

'Stephen said you'll be seeing him. Sooner than you think.'

Chapter Three
Chip-Boy Stephen

After school Todd was waiting for a bus with Louise and Lindy.

'How is old Wilson?' Louise asked.

'Not good,' Todd said. 'He's had a small stroke.'

'No!'

'Jason Ripley is on remand. He'll have to go to trial.'

'You'll be a witness?' Lindy asked.

'I got no choice,' Todd said.

Todd would have to go to court and point at Jason Ripley. The thought made him nervous. He wasn't afraid of Jason Ripley. He just wanted to do it right. A red Ford pulled up across the road. A big lad got out and marched up to them.

'You Todd Lucas?' he demanded.

Todd knew him. He worked in the chip shop near the library.

'I'm Stephen Ripley. You grassed

my brother up!'

Todd moved his feet so that they were apart.

'So?' he said.

A car door slammed. Someone else got out of the Ford. A tall kid. He had something in his hand. A table leg.

'Oh no,' Louise said.

'Can't get yourself a nice white girlfriend?' Stephen Ripley said.

Some of the other kids at the bus-stop laughed. That was it. It was one thing them having a go at Todd. But not at his mates.

Todd gave the lad a big shove. He

fell back on to the pavement. Then, quick as a flash, Todd pushed the boy over. He held his arm up his back. The other lad held the table leg up in the air.

'Touch me with that and I'll break his arm,' Todd said.

Todd pushed at the arm. The other lad stepped back.

'Don't threaten me,' Todd said. 'I don't grass on no one but your brother picked on an old man.'

Todd stood up. Ripley got to his feet.

'You'll see me again, Lucas!' Ripley shouted.

'Can't wait. Bring us a portion of chips next time!' Todd said.

The Ford drove off. Louise put her arm through his.

'You're shaking,' she said. She planted a kiss on his cheek. Todd felt himself go red. The bus appeared. He gave Louise a weak smile as he stepped on. Inside he wasn't feeling good. He would see Stephen Ripley again, he was sure.

Chapter Four
Attacked

Todd's mobile rang. He hoped it wasn't Louise. She kept sending him three or four texts every night. It was driving him mad.

He looked at the display.

It was Dex.

'I'm not going to school today,'
Dex said. 'We need to talk. Can you
come round?'

'Sure.'

It was twenty past nine. Todd had
time to go to Dex's house and still
get in for period two. His form tutor
would never know.

Dex opened his
front door. He had a
black eye and his
shirt was ripped.

'What happened?'
Todd said.

But Todd didn't

27

need an answer. He knew what had happened.

Stephen Ripley.

'What happened?' Todd said again. They were in Dex's room. Dex put his finger on his lips. He closed his room door.

'I told my mum I fell over,' he explained. 'I went out early to get milk. There was no one about. I was walking past the park entrance. Two lads jumped out in front of me.'

Dex picked up a small blue inhaler and puffed into his mouth. 'I only really saw the one in front. A big heavy kid with a funny eye.'

Stephen Ripley.

'He punched me in the face and took my mobile. He said, "Tell Todd Lucas I'll be giving him a call." '

Todd swore. He walked up and down Dex's room. He should have known that Ripley wouldn't leave it. He should have known!

Just then Todd's ring tone sounded. He pulled his mobile out. On the screen was the word Dex. Ripley was using Dex's mobile to call him. He answered it.

'What?'

'That's not a nice way to speak to someone!' said Ripley.

'What do you want?' Todd said.

'I had a chat with your friend this morning.'

'And?' Todd didn't trust himself to say more.

'I don't want my brother to go to prison. You have to withdraw your statement. Then I'll give your dwarf mate his mobile back.'

'You can chuck the mobile,' Todd said. 'There's plenty more where that came from.'

'I gave your mate a thump today,' Ripley said. 'Next, I'll break his legs.'

'Then you'll have me to deal with,' Todd said.

'You can't babysit your mate all the time. One night, weeks from now, when you and the dwarf think it's all over, I'll break his legs.'

Todd cut off the call.

'What did he say?' Dex asked.

'He wants me to withdraw my statement to the police.'

'You can't do that!' Dex said.

Todd didn't know what to do. He knew that Ripley was right. Todd couldn't be with Dex all the time. Poor Dex would have to pay for something Todd had done.

'Are you going to school?' Dex said.

Todd shook his head.

'I'm going to the police station.'

'You can't!' Dex said. 'We could report it to the police!'

'It would be his word against yours. I've decided. I'm going to withdraw my statement.'

Chapter Five
A Change of Heart

Todd walked to the police station.
At the corner he heard a voice.

'Todd!'

It was Louise. That girl had radar
for him. Her hair was up. It looked

good. She held a camcorder.

'Where you off to?' she said.

'What you doing with that?' he said, ignoring her question.

'Making footage of the streets. It's for our film. It's an advert for the area.'

Louise kept walking with him. When they got close to the police station, she put her hand on his arm.

'What you doing?' she said.

'I'm changing my statement. Ripley hit Dex and took his mobile. He's threatened to do worse.'

'But you can't. Jason Ripley will get off.'

'Maybe not. Mr Wilson saw him as well. When he's better he can identify him. This way, Dex won't get bothered.'

He walked into the station. Louise was still behind him. He stopped.

'Louise, I can do this on my own.'

'I'll wait out here. I'll take some film of the police station.'

'I might be a long time.'

'Don't matter. I'll wait,' she said.

He went in and stood at the counter.

'Is PC Roberts in?' he said.

Just then, PC Roberts walked into the public area. He looked unhappy. Todd called his name.

'I haven't got much time,' the PC said. 'I've just had a phone call from the hospital. George Wilson has died. He had a second stroke this morning.'

'Dead?' Todd said, shocked.

'I'm off to speak to his family. What can I do for you?'

'It's not important now,' said Todd.

He watched as the policeman walked off. The old man was dead. How could Todd change his story?

Todd told Louise everything.

Louise said, 'Can't you just beat up Stephen Ripley?'

'I could fight him,' Todd said. 'I could hurt him. But he could still get Dex.'

'Tell PC Roberts. He'll know what to do!'

'I got no evidence. It's Dex's word against Ripley!'

'When's his brother go to court?'

'A couple of weeks, I think. But now that Mr Wilson has died they might charge him again. He could be in court any day. Maybe even tomorrow.'

Louise went quiet for once. Todd's mind was racing. What could he do? Now Mr Wilson was dead, he couldn't withdraw his statement. But how could he get Stephen Ripley to leave Dex alone?

'Which chip shop does Ripley work in?' Louise said.

'The Mermaid,' Todd said

'Across from the library?'

Todd nodded. He wasn't sure why

she was asking.

'I've got an idea,' she said. 'Maybe we can trap the chip-shop boy.'

After school Todd walked to Dex's house. He was on his own. Louise said it was best that way. He thought about what he was going to say. Dex would agree to anything he asked. But could Todd ask him to put himself in such danger?

''Course I'll do it,' said Dex. 'You should have told me what Ripley said about breaking my legs. I'm not a baby.'

'I know,' Todd said. 'I just

thought...'

'Just because I got beat up, don't think that I'm a coward. I'm not.'

'I know you're not. I never said you were.'

Dex had sticky tape round the arm of his glasses. But there was a new hardness about him.

'I can't believe Mr Wilson's dead.'

Todd nodded. Dex took a puff of his blue inhaler. After a moment he exhaled.

'When are we going to do it?'

'Louise will check that Ripley's working in the shop tonight. She'll text me. Then we'll go about seven.

When it's dark.'

'No problem!' Dex said, cheerfully.

Later, Todd saw Dex put a
baseball bat in his bag. It gave him
a bad feeling.

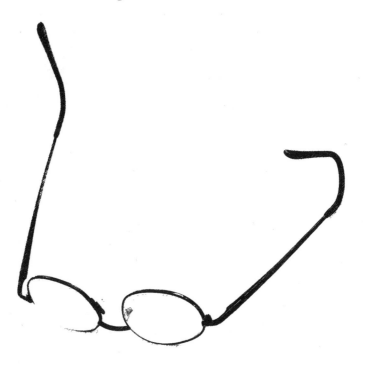

Chapter Six
Chip-Boy In Place

The Mermaid fish shop was lit up brightly. He gave Louise a call. She and Lindy were already there.

'I'll ring you as soon as something happens,' he said.

'Is Dex up for it?' she said.

'I think so,' Todd said. He pictured the baseball bat in Dex's bag. It made him nervous.

'OK. I'll wait to hear from you.'

Todd followed Dex along the shopping precinct. He stopped behind a van that was parked outside the shop. Dex walked in and stood by the counter.

Would Dex have the courage to confront Stephen Ripley? Todd felt weak and light-headed. It was a stupid plan. They were four fifteen-year-olds playing at being grown up.

Dex appeared at the door of the

shop. Then he ran along the pavement towards the end of the row of shops. Stephen Ripley flew out of the shop door after him. He was still wearing his overall. He was shouting something.

Todd felt panicky. There was no time to call it off. He made a quick call to Louise. Then he ran in the opposite direction. At the end of the shops he slowed down.

Todd walked quietly, his heart thumping. Further up he saw the white overall of Stephen Ripley. He hoped that Louise and Lindy were well hidden. He hoped that Dex had stopped running at the right place.

There was so much that could go wrong!

Todd crept along the alley with his back to the wall. He could hear Ripley shouting and swearing at Dex. Todd got as close as he could. He hid behind a dustbin. He could see what was happening.

'You won't break my legs,' Dex said, loudly. 'I'll break your legs. With this!'

Dex held the baseball bat high. He looked like he was waiting for someone to throw a ball at him. Ripley laughed. He jumped on Dex.

He grabbed the bat by its other end and pulled it off Dex.

'You can threaten Todd all you like,' Dex cried. 'He's not going to withdraw his statement. Your brother's going to prison.'

'I'll tell you what, dwarf! Jason said to just break one of your legs tonight. Then, if your mate doesn't change his statement, I'll come back and break the other one tomorrow!'

Todd looked hard into the darkness beyond Ripley. He could just see the very top of Louise's hair above the wheelie bin. This had to work. It had to work.

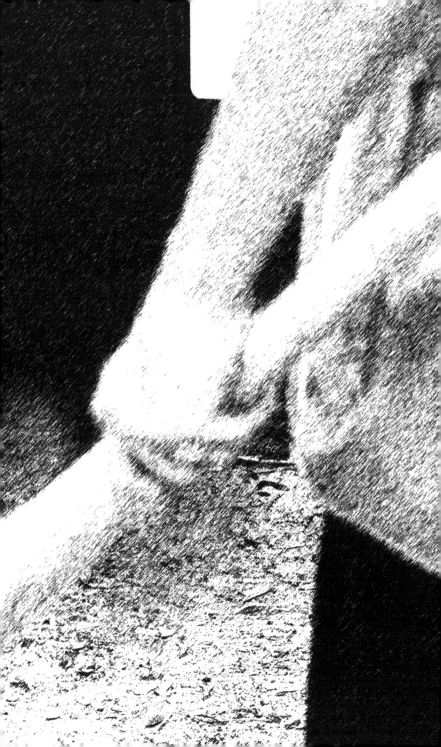

Dex didn't stop.

'You're a coward. You won't do it.'

Stephen Ripley swore and lifted the baseball bat. He swung it behind his head. Dex cried out in agony, as if he'd been hit. The bat swung down. Todd let out a loud whistle. Ripley missed Dex. The bat hit the wall. He turned around. There was Todd and the two girls. Each girl held a camcorder.

'Smile, Ripley,' Todd said. 'You're a movie star.'

Chapter Seven
Movie Star

They took the film to the police
station. PC Roberts took them into
a back office.

PC Roberts watched carefully.
The screen was filled with Ripley's

face. He was holding something in the air. It was hard to see what it was. Todd groaned. He put his head in his hands. Had it all been for nothing?

'Well, well!' PC Roberts said, pressing the STILL button.

Stephen Ripley looked like an alien. His face was recognisable. Just.

PC Roberts pushed the PLAY button. The film played on. They heard Ripley say, 'Jason said to just break one of your legs tonight. Then if your mate doesn't change his statement, I'll come back

and break the other one tomorrow.'

'That's interfering with witnesses,' Todd said, excitedly.

'You can arrest him for that? Can't you?' Louise said.

PC Roberts sat looking thoughtful.

'Strictly speaking he's not interfering with witnesses. Dexter here was not a witness to anything.'

Todd was angry. 'He beats up Dex and gets away with it!'

'No. It's threatening behaviour. Stephen Ripley has done this before. I was in court with him a month ago. The magistrate said it was his last chance.

He'll get a custodial sentence
this time.'

Todd left the station feeling better
than he had for days. Dex was
with Lindy. He looked taller. He
was walking fast, his hands swinging
at his sides. The baseball bat had
been a nice touch. Dex didn't take
it to protect himself. He always
meant Ripley to take it off him.

'You did a great job with the film,'
Todd told Louise.

'OK. I deserve a kiss then!' she
said.

Todd felt himself go red. He

stopped walking and gave her a kiss on the lips. Louise looked like she'd just won a prize.

Later, the four stopped outside Wilson's Food and Wines. The shutters were down. There was a notice pinned on the door.

We are closed due to the sad loss of George Wilson. Many thanks for the flowers and sympathy.

Louise held a bunch of carnations. She placed it on the pavement in front of the shop. The four stood quietly for a minute. Then they walked back towards school. Todd looked at his watch. With a bit of luck, he wouldn't be late. For once.

DOING THE DOUBLE

Alan Durant

Doing the Double

Dale and I used to play this game. We called it *Doing the Double*. If a team wins the league and cup, then they do the double. When we did the double, we pretended to be each other. Twins do it to trick people. For a joke.

We hadn't done it for years. But this time it was serious. Really serious...

At that moment I hated football more than ever.

A MURDER
OF CROWS

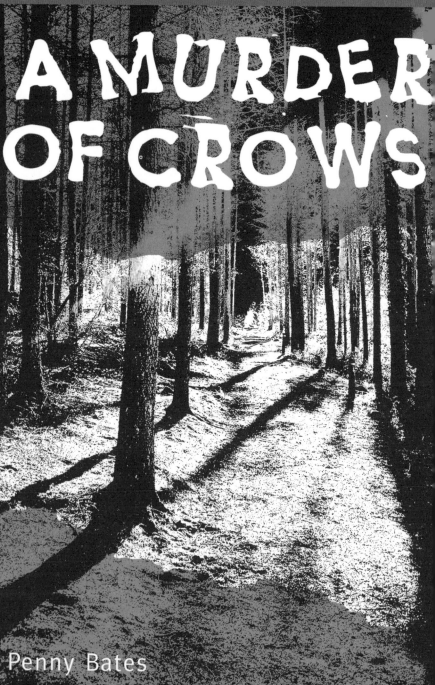

Penny Bates

A Murder of Crows

Some people said there was no such thing as Crow Law.

'It's survival of the fittest,' his daughter said. 'A sick crow is a danger to the flock. So the others finish it off.'

The old man knew better. There were many trials on Crow Hill. Many small skulls lay beneath the trees. It was the way of crows. They always cast out bad blood.

One crow stood on each side of the bird. They pecked out its eyes. Then the rest of the crows dived down. The crow's skull was pecked bare.

'It's not survival of the fittest,' the old man said. 'It's revenge!'

BLITZ

David Orme

Blitz

The shops on the Cut had their windows
blown in. People were sweeping up glass
and shovelling it into buckets. A copper
looked me up and down. There weren't
many kids in London in 1940. Most of them
were safely out in the country, eating bacon
and eggs for breakfast. Sensible kids, not
stupid ones like me.

At last I turned into Harrow Street.
The school was still there. The houses
opposite weren't. No number 18. And no
Aunt Josie. And Aunt Josie had never
believed in shelters.